Teddy Moffle's Hug

Mikenda Plant

Copyright © 2024 by Mikenda Plant

Mikenda Plant has asserted her right under the Copyright, Designs and Patents Act 1988 to be identified as the author of this work.

Apart from any fair dealing for the purposes of research or private study, or criticism or review, this publication may only be reproduced, stored or transmitted, in any form or by any means, with the prior permission in writing of the publishers, or in the case of reprographic reproduction in accordance with the terms of licenses issued by the Copyright Licensing Agency. Enquiries concerning reproduction outside those terms should be sent to the publishers.

This is a work of fiction. Names, characters, businesses, places, events and incidents are either the products of the author's imagination or used in a fictitious manner. Any resemblance to actual persons, living or dead, or actual events is purely coincidental.

First published in UK by Moffle Press

Web: www.moffles.com
Twitter & Instagram: @themoffles

ISBN 978-1-7384648-0-7

British Library Cataloguing in Publication Data.
A CIP catalogue record for this book is available from the British Library.

First edition printed February 2024
All rights reserved. Printed in the UK

For Gerard, Kian and Marshal.

Have you ever seen a Moffle? Moffles are tiny, fast and fluffy. It is hard to spot one, as they can move so quickly and quietly.

Some have curly fur and some have straight fur. Some are soft and silky and some are wiry and frizzy.

An amazing thing about Moffles is that they show their emotions in their fur.

When they are happy they glow yellow. When they are angry they simmer red. When they are scared, their fur turns a certain shade of purple, and when they are sad it goes blue.

All baby Moffles are born with their hearts full of love to give and the Moffle colour of love is pink.

Moffles have many adventures and all the colours of their emotions stay with them in their fur, for the world to read like a story book. You can always tell an old Moffle who has led a full life, as their fur will be a patchwork of all the feelings it has ever had.

There are lots of Moffles with stories to tell and this is the story of Teddy Moffle's hug.

Teddy Moffle has moved to another home again.
Everything's new and different for you.
I wonder if you're feeling scared?
Would you like a hug?

No - I'm tough!

Thanks for letting me know. Even though your little paws are shaking, you're telling me you're tough. You've had to be for such a long time.

The hugs are here if you need them, but only when you're ready, Teddy.

No - I'm tough!

Thanks for letting me know. Even though your little ears are drooping, you're telling me you're tough. It's hard to move so many times and have to make new friends.

The hugs are here if you need them, but only when you're ready, Teddy.

Teddy Moffle is scampering in the snow.

You forgot your hat and look very cold.

Would you like a hug?

No - I'm tough!

Thanks for letting me know. Even though your little body is shivering, you're telling me you're tough. Maybe you've never had someone before who cares about keeping you warm.

The hugs are here when you need them, but only when you're ready, Teddy.

Teddy Moffle has fallen over.

Ouch! That was a big fall right on your nose! Would you like a hug?

No - I'm tough!

Thank you for letting me know. Even though your little whiskers are quivering, you're telling me you're tough. I wonder where the hurt feelings go?

The hugs are here if you need them, but only when you're ready, Teddy.

Teddy Moffle has had a bad dream.

It's OK, I've turned on the light, and I'm right here for you. Would you like a hug?

No - I'm tough!

Thanks for letting me know. Even though I heard you squeak, you're telling me you're tough. It might take some time for you to trust me, I know your heart's been hurt.

The hugs are here if you need them, but only when you're ready, Teddy.

Teddy Moffle is at a theme park.
So many bright lights and lots of noise!
Would you like a hug?

Thanks for letting me know. Even though your furry face seems nervous, you're telling me you're tough. You've looked out for yourself for so long.

The hugs are here if you need them, but only when you're ready, Teddy.

Teddy Moffle drops his candy floss.

Oops - butter paws! It was just an accident. Would you like another one?

I saw the worry on your fluffy green tummy - thanks for letting me know.

Teddy Moffle goes on the log flume.

You're getting splashed but you have such a big smile!

Yes, it's fun!

Your yellow cheeks are telling me that - thanks for letting me know.

Teddy Moffle is in the Haunted House.

Ooh it's dark and spooky. Would you like a hug?

Hold my paw - that will be enough!

Your squeeze of my paw says, 'when you're close, I feel braver'. Thanks for letting me know.

Teddy Moffle rides on the Big Dipper.

Up, up, up to the very top.

Waiting to drop…

Teddy Moffle has a big hug.

And plenty more where that came from.
We never run out of hugs!

Mikenda Plant is a Family Therapist from Nottingham, UK. When she isn't drawing Moffles, some things she likes doing are riding her bike, photography and playing with her cat, Martha.

If you like Teddy Moffle, you can find more Moffle stories, colouring pictures & activities that are free for you to enjoy from the Moffle website: www.moffles.com

And you can follow us on Facebook & Instagram @themoffles

'Tippy Moffle's Mirror' and 'Billy Moffle's Straight Lines' are available to buy online at the Moffle website & other online book retailers.